D0041555

WEDNESDAY WILSON

GETS DOWN TO BUSINESS

To my kids, who lent their voices and experiences to help bring Wednesday to life, and to all the kids like them who aren't afraid to speak their minds. This is for you! — B.G.

Text © 2021 Bree Galbraith
Illustrations © 2021 Morgan Goble

All rights reserved. No part of this publication may be reproduced, stored in a retrieval system or transmitted, in any form or by any means, without the prior written permission of Kids Can Press Ltd. or, in case of photocopying or other reprographic copying, a license from The Canadian Copyright Licensing Agency (Access Copyright). For an Access Copyright license, visit www.accesscopyright.ca or call toll free to 1-800-893-5777.

Published in Canada and the U.S. by Kids Can Press Ltd.
25 Dockside Drive, Toronto, ON M5A 0B5

Kids Can Press is a Corus Entertainment Inc. company

www.kidscanpress.com

The artwork in this book was rendered digitally.
The text is set in Baskerville.

Edited by Katie Scott
Designed by Andrew Dupuis

Printed and bound in Shenzhen, China, in 10/2020 by C & C Offset

CM 21 0 9 8 7 6 5 4 3 2 1

Library and Archives Canada Cataloguing in Publication

Title: Wednesday Wilson gets down to business / written by Bree Galbraith ; illustrated by Morgan Goble.

Names: Galbraith, Bree, author. | Goble, Morgan, 1996– illustrator.

Identifiers: Canadiana 20200290134 | ISBN 9781525303272 (hardcover)

Classification: LCC PS8613.A4592 W43 2021 | DDC jC813/.6 — dc23

Kids Can Press gratefully acknowledges that the land on which our office is located is the traditional territory of many nations, including the Mississaugas of the Credit, the Anishnabeg, the Chippewa, the Haudenosaunee and the Wendat peoples, and is now home to many diverse First Nations, Inuit and Métis peoples.

We thank the Government of Ontario, through Ontario Creates; the Ontario Arts Council; the Canada Council for the Arts; and the Government of Canada for supporting our publishing activity.

WEDNESDAY WILSON
GETS DOWN TO BUSINESS

Written by BREE GALBRAITH
Illustrated by MORGAN GOBLE

KIDS CAN PRESS

CONTENTS

CHAPTER 0
The Five Most Important Things about Me

There are several important things you should know about me before reading my book. Usually I charge a dollar for this information, but for a limited time only, it's free.

1. My name is Wednesday August Wilson. But you can call me Wednesday. I was supposed to be born on a Friday in September, but instead I was born on a Wednesday in August. My moms hadn't picked a name yet.

2. I have two moms (a mom and a mum, to be precise), which is confusing for some people but not when they get to know me. Some people ask which one is my real mom, because I'm mixed race and I don't look exactly like either one of them. Lately I've stopped answering, because clearly they're both real! And really, it's no one's business, right?

3. I have a little brother named Mister. Our moms let him change his name last year because he stopped listening when people called him (especially his preschool teacher, Ms. Hill). At first, everyone thought he had a hearing problem, so they took him to a ton of ear specialists. But it turned out he just didn't like his name anymore. When our moms said he could change it, he first chose the name Moo. "We're not calling you Moo, mister," my mum said. And that's how he got the idea to go by Mister.

4. My best friend is Charlie Lopez. We have been friends since we were two weeks old. We hang out a minimum of nine times a week, not including recess and lunch, or when he's at swimming lessons or his dad's house for the weekend. It would be even more, but our teacher, Ms. Gelson, doesn't group our desks together anymore because we talk too much. I'm 82 percent sure she has

superhuman hearing, because even when we whisper, she can still hear us.

5. THE MOST IMPORTANT THING: I'm going to be an entrepreneur. It's a hard word to say for something so simple, but it sounds like this: *on-tra-pren-ur*. It's basically a fancy word for someone who runs their own business and makes tons of money. I haven't started any businesses yet, but I'm pretty sure today is the day. That's why I'm so excited you're reading this book — you get to know me before I make it big, so later when there's a movie about me, you could be interviewed and tell the director how nice I am.

Maybe you're reading this in class and the bell is about to ring, or you're at home before bed and your eyes are tired, so I have to get to the good stuff! Business! I've had a lot of business ideas floating around lately, which is a good thing because I have a big, long list of things I want to buy once I'm a successful entrepreneur. In fact, it's the longest list I have. (If I shared it all here, it would take a whole month just to read it.) At the top of my list is a surprise vacation for my family, so that we can come back from winter break with those tags on our jacket zippers that show people we went skiing. There's no end to my list because I keep adding to it.

MY BIG, LONG LIST
OF THINGS I WANT TO BUY

- surprise vacation for my family
- electric scooter to get to meetings
  (I don't have any yet, but I will)
- briefcase for my important papers that
  only opens with my fingerprints
- more vegetable boxes for the
  community garden
- new fridge for my mum's food truck
  because her fridge is always breaking down
- computer just for me that I don't have
  to share with Mister
- website to sell my products online,
  when I get around to having them
- puppy (even though I'm not allowed
  to get one)
- camouflage dog crate that my puppy
  can hide in

But if you think money is the only reason I want to start my own business, then you're wrong. I know from being a big sister that I'd make a good boss, since I'm really good at making rules (but not so good at following them). Plus, if you run your own company, you can bring your puppy to work!

WEDNESDAY WILSON

#1 BOSS

SEPTEMBER

CHAPTER 1
Business as Usual

I haven't decided which business to start
first, or what would make the most money.
I want enough to fill a vault so that I could
keep my money safe and also swim in it.
I have no idea how much a vault costs,
and when I tried to ask my mom, she told
me to make memories, not money. She's
an artist and hasn't sold a painting in at
least a year. When I asked her for business
advice, she said all she can teach me about
is perseverance, which is a fancy word for
"not giving up."

My mum, on the other hand, knows a ton about business. She gets up before sunrise to get the pizza ready for her food truck, the Teresaria. She only uses vegetables from the community garden, and her truck is the most popular in the city. At least I think it is.

Because Mum doesn't have any employees, she's usually not here in the morning — which means I mostly just eat my breakfast and try not to let Mister get on my nerves. If he and I argue too much, I don't get an allowance.

Mister and I each receive an allowance that's the exact same amount as our ages. I get three dollars more than him because I'm three years older. Mister mostly spends his allowance on art supplies. He wants to be an artist one day, like Mom. We stopped getting a regular allowance after my mom read an article about how kids shouldn't get paid to help around the house, they should just *do it*. Clearly the person who wrote the article was never a kid.

In order to get an allowance, I have to do helpful acts for *other* people, like:

- help my neighbor
  Mr. Wright carry his
  groceries inside
- feed my tutor
  Molly's cat when she
  goes skiing

If you didn't already notice, I like to make lists. Successful people make lists to organize all of their amazing thoughts, so obviously I make tons of them.

GOOD THINGS ABOUT MY ALLOWANCE

- I've been getting really good at saving. Charlie rigged my piggy bank so the coins fall into a secret compartment in the pig's butt where even I forget to look.
- When I help Mr. Wright with his groceries, he gives me the kind of sugary cookies my moms won't buy.

BAD THINGS ABOUT MY ALLOWANCE

- It doesn't go up by fifty cents on my half-birthday, because my mum said that's not even a thing.
- I think Molly's cat is out to get me.

So far I've saved $31.50 in my piggy bank's butt. I don't know about you, but where I live, that is NOT enough to buy anything on my list. But it's a start, right? On the way to school today, Charlie is going to help me figure out which of my business ideas could make REAL money.

SECReT SAVINGS

MONeY GOeS heRe

*SMASh to eMPTY

CHAPTER 2
Mind Your Business

A lot of people think Charlie is just a regular guy with a bajillion freckles, but that's because he's shy and doesn't show people his skills. He's planning on being an inventor. He also knows a ton of facts because his mom writes those *1000 Weirdest Things on the Planet* books. He's the perfect person to help me start a business because he has the type of brain that thinks about the tiny details. One day I'll make him my Vice President of Operations.

Our school, Harbor View Elementary, is right around the corner. It's so close that we can hear the bell from both of our houses, and at mine, it's louder. But we take a different route to school every day for two reasons:

1. to avoid certain people (which I'll explain later)
2. so that a spy trying to steal* our top-secret inventions wouldn't be able to follow us

*Just so you know, inventions aren't safe until they have a patent, which is basically an official letter from the government saying no one can copy you. But patents cost money, so I should add that to my big, long list of things I want to buy.

Every morning since school started a few weeks ago, we decide which route to take to get there. This morning we're taking the long route because we need all the time we can get to write down the business ideas I've had. Mister doesn't have a say in the route, plus we have a no-fighting-on-the-way-to-school rule, so we go my way.

"I should take notes because I'm great at making lists and I have a clipboard," I say to Charlie.

"True," he replies. "Plus you're better at walking and writing at the same time."

"Double true," I say. "And you're much more of a 3D thinker."

"Triple true," he says. But this could go on forever, so I write the title in big letters and underline it. Then I start writing down all the ideas I have, and we even add a few more.

BUSINESSES WE CAN START TODAY (WITHOUT A LOT OF OVERHEAD*)

- lemonade stand
  (check fridge for lemons
  after school)
- dog walking
  (I'd walk my dog for
  free if I had one)
- toy sale

- car wash
- cutting grass
- portrait stand
  (Mister's idea)
- catching crickets
  (Charlie's idea)

*Overhead is a business term for the money it takes to run a business, which I don't have a lot of, because I only have $31.50 saved in my piggy bank's butt.

We stop our list right there, but not because we want to. I told you I'd explain later why we take a different route to school every day, and I suppose now's a good time ... Meet Ruby Beautiful.

CHAPTER 2 ½

Ruby Beautiful and the Emmas

Ruby's house is just like mine, and it's directly across the courtyard, so it's like her house stares at my house, giving it bad looks. She's in fourth grade, but she's in the same class as me and Charlie, even though we're in third grade, because it's a split class. Ms. Gelson sits me and Ruby together and puts us in the same silent reading group because we *don't* talk. Ruby used to be best friends with me and Charlie, but then over the summer the Emmas started calling her Ruby Beautiful and she decided to become friends with them — including my archnemesis, Emma M. I haven't asked her yet why she stopped being my friend.

Part of me likes having an archnemesis, but another part wishes it wasn't Ruby's new best friend. My mom said Ruby's going through a phase. I hope so. I also hope I don't catch a phase — it seems to make you evil.

Ruby's new group of friends follow Emma M. around like puppies on invisible leashes. We call them the Emmas, even though one is actually named Emmet.

Their full names are Emma Meng, Emmet Easton, Emma Arseneau and Emma Nicks, but we just use their last initials to tell them apart. I don't think it's a coincidence that their last initials spell *M.E.A.N.*

Emma
M.

Emmet
E.

Emma
A.

Emma
N.

Ruby Beautiful and the Emmas are the number one reason we take a different route to school each morning. But sometimes we can't avoid them. And this is one of those mornings.

"What weird things are you two up to now?" Emma M. asks before we have a chance to make a detour. I was too busy walking and writing to notice the Emmas behind us. Mister, who is supposed to be on Emma-alert, wasn't paying attention.

"It's nothing," Charlie mutters.

"Just tell us what you're writing about," says Emma A. I haven't heard her talk before, so I must look pretty surprised.

In my head, she uses telepathy to tell the other Emmas what she's thinking.

"Ummmm … it's just a list," I answer to no one in particular.

"Can I see it?" asks Ruby. She seems excited for a second but then tries not to let it show. The Emmas definitely have her under some kind of spell.

And then the absolute worst thing happens. Emma M. grabs the list from my clipboard and begins to read it out loud.

"*A lemonade stand.*" She rolls her eyes. "How original."

When she's done, they all laugh, even though nothing on the list is remotely funny. Well, except maybe the "catching crickets" part. But Charlie's sister has a pet tarantula and pays Charlie a nickel for every cricket he catches to feed it.

"Come on, Wednesday," says Mister, tugging at my jacket. "Let's go."

Ruby takes the list and hands it back to me. But not before the Emmas all laugh at us again.

"I knew it was going to be weird!" Emma M. says. "Who's gonna buy lemonade from a bunch of cricket catchers?!"

"Ewww," they all groan at the same time.

When they finally leave, Charlie tells me a fact. He does that when he gets stressed out. I think it calms him down, but it also makes me smarter. So it's win-win, as my moms would say.

"Did you know that a howler monkey's groan can be heard three miles away?"

"Really?" I answer. "I bet the Emmas are louder!"

We all laugh, especially Mister. And then we run because we hear the first school bell. The rest of the list will have to wait until recess.

CHAPTER 3
The Kale Incident

The best thing about my classroom (besides Charlie) is Morten. He's a bearded dragon, which is a kind of lizard. Ms. Gelson's son donated him to the class after going away to university. On the days we don't have art or gym, Morten is the main reason I want to go to school.

At night, he sleeps in a giant terrarium next to my desk, but during class, you can sign him out and put his harness on, then attach his leash to your desk. You can only take him out when everyone's doing a quiet activity, like journal writing, or else he gets too excited and poops on the floor. Ms. Gelson lets me write him letters instead of journaling because it's much easier to write to Morten than to try to remember interesting details about my life. Especially when we're not supposed to make up stuff in our journals.

Since it's Monday morning, we're doing our "weekend reflection." It rained all weekend, so I don't have much to reflect on. I start the way I always do:

Dear Morten,

Today me and Charlie are making a list of business ideas. He thinks we should catch crickets for people with tarantulas, but I don't think many people have spiders for pets. They mostly have dogs (lucky) and cats.

I don't know much about pets other than the fact that Molly's cat food smells like rotten feet. And that your favorite food is kale. My mum puts kale on one of the pizzas in her food truck. It tastes as awful as it sounds and never sells out so she always packs it in my lunch. Charlie gets a sandwich in his lunch every day. But never with peanut butter because Randall is anafilacktic. I don't want to scare you but that means he could die if he eats peanuts.

Your friend,

Wednesday

When I'm done my letter, I trace over the words to make it look like I'm still writing until at least three other people are done, too. When people start using pencil crayons, I know they are drawing pictures in their journals and that it's safe to stop pretending to write. Then I sign out Morten, tuck my letter under his harness and point him toward Ms. Gelson's desk. It's how I always hand in my weekend reflection.

"Morten meanders merrily on a masterful mission," Ms. Gelson once said. She always makes things fun, even words.

I start getting bored just sitting there, and I always get my best business ideas when I'm bored, so then I get really excited.

I'm so bored my eyes start drooping and my head gets floppy. I know a good idea is coming — I can just *feel* it. I need to talk to Charlie now, because I know that my great idea will pop out when we're together.

I stare at the back of Charlie's head and say his name in my mind at least a hundred times. I haven't mastered telepathy yet like the Emmas, and he doesn't turn around. I consider sending him a note on Morten's back, but Morten is still on his way to Ms. Gelson. Can I wait until recess? I don't think so, because we still have to get through a math lesson, so I have to pay attention and have no time for getting bored. I have to talk to him now.

I pretend like I need my water bottle and head to the cubbies.

"Charlie!" I whisper as I pass by his desk. "H-2-O!"

He knows that's the code to meet at the cubbies. Charlie and I leave our water bottles in our backpacks so we have an excuse to go to the cubbies, which have a dividing wall so no one can see us. Ms. Gelson says we never have to ask to get water, so it's the perfect desk-escape plan.

Once we're safely at the cubbies, I tell Charlie that I can feel a great idea coming on. The only thing is, he isn't as excited as I thought he would be.

"Wednesday," whispers Charlie, "you have to come up with an idea *before* calling a meeting with me." Charlie is very practical like that. I'll tell you more later, but sometimes I'm not as practical and can't help making bad decisions.

"But it's on the tip of my tongue!" I assure him.

"Okay, fine," he says, pulling out his invention notebook that's filled with graph paper.

Then out of the corner of my eye, I notice Morten turn his head to me instead of toward Ms. Gelson's desk.

"No! Morten!" I say, waving my arms back and forth. But this only makes Morten more interested. "He's going to draw attention to us."

"Throw something near Ms. Gelson's desk!" Charlie says.

"Good idea!" I say, and I reach into my lunch bag and pull out the leftover pizza. I rip the kale off the top and flick it toward the desk. The kale travels surprisingly far but hits Lamar's desk instead, sticking to the side. I try again.

Flick goes the kale. It leaves my fingertips just as Emma M. leans down to pick up her pencil from the floor. Charlie and I watch in horror as the kale lands right on Emma's cheek.

It sticks there for the longest second in the history of time before she wipes it away in disgust. A tomatoey smudge stays behind. Emma's eyes widen with anger as she looks around the classroom for the culprit. Charlie and I are frozen in amazement. I mean fear. Fearmazement.

"I never knew kale could travel that far," whispers Charlie. "I'll take note of that."

Then Emma M. spots us.

"We're doomed," I say.

"Caught red-handed," says Charlie, looking down at my pizza-sauced fingers.

"It's been nice knowing you," I say as we watch Emma M. coming our way. She's already used her telepathic skills to alert

Ruby and the other Emmas, who follow behind her.

"Should we run?" I ask. But it's no use. Charlie is still frozen, and they have us surrounded.

CHAPTER 4
Not So Secret

"You have five seconds to explain yourselves," says Emma M. "And if we don't like what we hear, we're telling Ms. Gelson as soon as she calls us all back to our desks."

This is bad on so many levels. First of all, the Emmas can get you in trouble just for sneezing. And second of all, I pretty much have zero chances left right now. As Mom said last month, there are already two strikes against me.

I may as well tell you about how I can't help making decisions without thinking things through completely — I usually think of what can go right, not wrong. My mum says it's "how I'm wired" and that seeing the potential in things will make me a great entrepreneur. But if something does go wrong, my moms always find out.

The first strike happened after I put water down the slide at the park (which makes it go a lot faster, by the way). The second strike was when I was working on my self-portrait assignment for art class. I by accident photocopied my face three hundred times instead of just once using the scanner in Mum's office.

Last week, after the scanner situation, Mom told me that a third strike means

I'm grounded for a whole week without negotiation* so I have time to think about the consequences of my actions.

If you think that was all the bad stuff, you're wrong. Because if I'm grounded that means I can't hang out with Charlie after school, and then how are we ever going to get our business off the ground?

So I need to do everything I can right now to stay out of trouble.

Charlie shifts around nervously, which is never a good sign.

"For every human in the world, there are one million ants!" he blurts out.

*Negotiation is an important business skill, so if I do get grounded, I'm planning to negotiate it down to three days.

Ruby sighs, but the Emmas stare at Charlie ferociously. His cheeks turn bright red. Redder than his hair, redder than the pizza sauce still stuck to Emma M.'s cheek, *so red* his freckles have almost disappeared.

"I'm sorry, Emma," I say, standing in front of Charlie to shield him from her death glare. "It was an accident — I was aiming for Morten. Please don't tell on us … Charlie was helping me with a business idea, and we don't have time to get in trouble. I'll — I'll do your homework for a week!"

"Emma M. doesn't have homework, Wednesday," says Emmet, putting his arm around her. "We use *our* class time wisely. Try again."

I don't know how the Emmas get such good grades when all they do is pass notes all day long. Then Ruby looks like she's going to say something, and I brace myself for the worst.

"What's your idea?" Ruby asks. And she actually seems interested. We used to invent things together, but now the Emmas tease us that it's something only little kids do. All of a sudden, I'm embarrassed that we don't have a cool idea to prove them wrong.

Charlie begins to speak. "It's, it's a —"

"Secret!" I say suddenly. Everyone looks at me.

I'm sure you know that when you say something's a secret, it's because you don't really have anything to say. The Emmas look at each other and start to laugh. Then Emma M. holds her cheek in her hand and says she's feeling faint. Emma N. mentions the school nurse has ice packs for injuries like this, but they would have to tell him everything that happened. The only good thing about Emma M. going to the nurse is that she'd be given the same ice pack that Randall had on his butt after sitting on his pencil last week. I try really hard not to laugh. Charlie can't even look me in the eye. Now what? *Think, Wednesday. THINK!*

"It's a secret … *keeper*," I blurt out, and suddenly everyone seems very interested. I flip through Charlie's invention notebook so fast they can't see what's on the pages. "And if you don't tell on us, you can have the first one on the house."

"What does that mean?" Emma N. asks.

"It means for free."

"I know *that*, Wednesday," she says, rolling her eyes. "I mean, what's a *Secret Keeper*?"

Now's my chance to share my elevator pitch*! "A Secret Keeper," I start to say, hoping my brain can keep up with my mouth, "is the newest way to protect the things you need to keep a secret."

*An *elevator pitch* is another business thing where you pretend to be in an elevator with someone really rich who only has a few seconds to learn about your business so they can give your company money. My moms make us take the stairs all the time, so I'll probably never end up in an elevator with a rich person, but you get the idea.

"And it's portable!" adds Charlie.

They don't seem convinced. I'll have to try another angle.

"You know those notes you pass in class?" I say, and all the Emmas nod their heads. "Well, imagine if they fell into the wrong hands." I make a sideways glance at Ms. Gelson for effect.

The Emmas gasp. Emmet covers his face with his hands. They are so dramatic, and finally it works in my favor.

They look interested now. Ruby does, too.

Then Emma N. speaks. "Obviously that would never happen because, unlike some people, we are careful," she says, rolling her eyes at me. "But that doesn't mean we don't want one."

Ruby and the Emmas turn to huddle together and start whispering to each other before Emma M. finally turns to us. "We expect a Secret Keeper delivered to my desk before first bell tomorrow morning," she says, looking directly at me. "*Or else.*"

CHAPTER 5
Finding the Opportunity

The rest of the morning goes by in a blur. I don't even have time to get bored once with all the Secret Keeper thoughts running through my head. Charlie and I can't figure out if we're lucky to have our first customers or if we're in real trouble. Either way, we know the first thing we have to do when the recess bell rings is figure out how to make a Secret Keeper.

I watch the clock in the classroom, counting down the seconds. Five … four … three … two … *BRRRING*. Freedom!

Charlie and I don't waste any time. We grab our snacks and head straight to the kindergarten playground to find Mister. It's Charlie's idea, since he thinks Mister is really good at solving problems. I'm not convinced, but I agree just to keep Charlie happy — I need him as a business partner and a friend.

It's easy to spot Mister in the crowd because he's the only kindergartner reading a chapter book instead of swinging on the monkey bars. We fill him in on the problem. I mean, opportunity. My mum says when you think something is a problem, it has no choice but to be one. So instead you should think of it as an opportunity.

Once Mister knows exactly what
happened, he puts down his book and asks,
"What does *portable* mean?"

"It means you can take it with you,"
answers Charlie. I take out my clipboard
and start making a list.

SECRET KEEPER
1. hides secret things
2. portable (you can take it with you)

"Okay, great," says Mister. "So we need
to invent something that can store secrets,
that you can take with you and that can be
invented today."

"We have tonight, too," I add.
Opportunities, right?

"I have some sort-of-bad news," says Charlie, picking at the grass by his feet. "It's Monday …"

"… and I have to help Mr. Wright with his groceries at four-fifteen," I think out loud, worried we won't have enough time for inventing.

"And I can't stay long after that because I have swimming lessons," says Charlie. "I really have to pass this level or I will still be swimming with kindergartners. No offense, Mister."

"That's okay," says Mister, repositioning his glasses. "I know what you mean."

"Maybe," Charlie says, "given our limited time, we can repurpose something old instead of build something new."

"What does *repurpose* mean?" asks Mister. I don't know either, so I'm glad Mister isn't afraid to ask.

"*Repurpose* means to use something that already exists, but in a different way," explains Charlie.

"Well, then, we need to get repurposing ASAP," I tell them. "Or else I'm doomed!" To make sure they know how upset I am, I grab a handful of grass and throw it in the air as dramatically as I possibly can.

Charlie sneezes away the grass I threw, and a booger-covered four-leaf clover lands on my clipboard. We all laugh.

"Do you think a snotty clover is still good luck?" asks Charlie, wiping it off.

"Of course it is!" I tell him. "My mom says if you keep it somewhere safe, it will always bring you luck."

"You're the one who picked it," he says, handing it to me, "and sort of the one who needs it most."

The bell rings, and the kindergartners start to line up. I can't believe we haven't figured this out yet! I turn the clover around in my hand.

"I can keep that for you until we get home, Wednesday," says Mister, opening his book to the middle and holding it out for me. "You're supposed to flatten it safely in a book."

"THAT'S IT!" I yell so loud that a playground monitor notices we aren't in line yet and starts making his way over. With no time to spare, I tell Mister to meet me and Charlie in the library at lunch. Then I inhale my yogurt tube, and we run to our line as fast as we can. I think I found the opportunity!

CHAPTER 6
A New Hire

Back in class, I'm having a hard time sitting
still. It's even harder than usual, and not
just because we're working on spelling.
We're supposed to be writing sentences
that contain this week's spelling words,
which tie in with our lesson on stereotypes.
Ms. Gelson explained that *stereotype* means
when you assume something about other
people because of their age, skin color,
clothes, where they live, how much money
their family has or something like that. Like
how not all bullies are big and ugly, but
some are short and pretty.

Even though I know eight words are supposed to equal eight sentences, I can't help but try to shove them all into one sentence so I can move on to free time and plan out a Secret Keeper. Technically Ms. Gelson said, "Use each of these words in a sentence," so I'm not exactly wrong. I stare at the words:

Accept   Culture
Assumption   Differences
Conflict   Expect
Identical   Stereotype

After a few tries, I come up with a pretty good sentence and go to Ms. Gelson's desk so she can sign my work. I'm surprised that

I'm the first one there. Amina is usually at Ms. Gelson's desk before all of us, but this time she's right behind me. Amina's new to our school, and her work is always perfect. Lining up behind her isn't great, unless you like being compared to someone who never makes mistakes.

"Wednesday?" says Ms. Gelson. "You're ready to show me your sentences?"

I open my book. "Yep," I tell her. "I used all the words."

Ms. Gelson looks at the page and then back up at me. I smile, and half of her mouth smiles, too. She raises her eyebrows and starts reading.

"Stereotypes are making assumptions about people from the same culture or group and accepting that they are all identical but this makes conflict instead of expecting differences." My sentence sounds even better when she says it out loud.

Ms. Gelson says, "Hmm," which is never a good sign. "Well, I guess it fulfills the assignment," she starts, "but you mixed up two words in here."

I search the sentence, but I don't see what she's talking about. I say it back to myself a few times in my head.

"Ms. Gelson?" Amina says from behind me.

"Yes, Amina?"

Amina smiles at me.
"I *expect* to return my library book during free time. Will you *accept* Wednesday as my library buddy?"

Ms. Gelson laughs and turns back to me. "Wednesday, if you know the words you mixed up, you can start free time by accompanying Amina to the library."

I think about what Amina said. "*Expecting* that they are all identical instead of *accepting* differences!" I tell Ms. Gelson with a smile, and she gives us permission to leave.

When we're downstairs, I thank Amina and tell her it was really important for me to finish early.

"Do you need a new book, too?" she whispers as we enter the library. "I didn't know there were business books in our library." Amina smiles. Who knew Amina knew so much about me?

"I *do* need a book, but not to read. Can you keep a secret?" I ask, and Amina nods. "We're inventing a Secret Keeper."

"What's that, and who's 'we'? And why
would you want a book you won't read?"
Amina asks. She's standing on a stool,
trying to figure out which book to take
off the top shelf.

I look around to make sure we're alone. "Me, Charlie and Mister are the 'we,' but I can't tell you anything else right now because I'm still working it out in my head. If you want to join us, we're meeting here at lunchtime."

Amina gets down from the stool. "I'd love to come!"

"You're hired!" I say. Anyone who wants to run a business knows that you need smart people on your team. "Just eat lunch really fast," I tell her, "then come straight to the library. And don't bring anyone with you!"

"Don't worry," she says. "I usually eat lunch alone."

Now that I think about it, I haven't noticed as much about Amina as she has about me, which doesn't seem fair. Making friends when you're the new kid must be hard.

"Well, I'm glad you're working with us now," I tell her.

"Me, too," she says, and we head back to class.

CHAPTER 7
Logistics*

Charlie and I scarf down our lunches; then we book it to the library. Once Mister, Charlie and Amina are all around the table in the back of the library, I take a chapter book off the shelf and hold it out to them. Then to explain my idea, I pretend I'm pitching the invention to a group of investors.**

*A fancy word for having a plan

**Investors are people who have so much money that they actually like giving it away to help other people start companies.

"From the outside, this may look like an ordinary book," I explain, showing them the cover. "But when you open it, you realize it has a secret compartment that's been hollowed out. It's the perfect way to keep something secret from getting into the wrong hands."

"That's so cool!" says Amina. Charlie and Mister agree.

Charlie gets out his graph paper and sketches an idea.

Then I pull out my clipboard to list the supplies we'll need. I make a big title on a new piece of paper, and then I underline it twice.

SECRET KEEPER SUPPLIES:

- books
- scissors
- glue

"I have scissors and glue in my pencil case," says Amina, "but where are we going to find the books we need?"

This is one of those times when the answer seems so obvious to me (hello … we're sitting in the *library*) that it makes me wonder if it's a "red flag" that other people don't see it. But I don't see any red flag here. So I continue.

"Library books," I tell them. Charlie squirms in his seat. Mister's eyes open wide, and Amina slides her book into her bag. I can tell they need convincing. As the leader, it's my job to motivate everyone so they feel personally attached to the business. I read that in a magazine.

"What if we only use books that have stereotypes in them?" I ask them. "Ms. Gelson said stereotypes are bad, right? Charlie, are there any stereotypes you don't like in books?"

"I hate how in a lot of books, the boys are only good at sports and nothing else," he says. "Boys have more skills than just throwing a ball!"

"I hate that, too!" says Mister.

Amina tells us what kind of books she doesn't like. "I hate it when girl characters need to be saved by boys. Why can't the girl be the hero?"

Everyone agrees, and I let them know the opportunity we have at our fingertips. "How about we make Secret Keepers only out of the books that are filled with these stereotypes?"

The group looks a bit more hopeful. "And I will sign them all out on my library card." They nod but don't entirely agree. "And I will take the blame if anything goes wrong."

That last point has everyone agreeing,
so we get started, searching the shelves.

When we're done collecting, we lay
all the books out on the table. There are
twenty-two in total.

"What if someone wants to check one of these out in the future?" asks Charlie, looking at the stack.

I hold up one called *Rumor Rescue*. It has a football player on the cover carrying a crying cheerleader. We all agree that no one would miss this book.

I have to tell you that I don't sign out many books from the school library for two reasons:

1. There aren't any business books.
2. Until this year, the library was usually closed because our school didn't have enough money for a librarian (or new books).

I walk up to the circulation desk, where our new librarian, Ms. Eleanor, is frantically trying to sign in all of the returns before the bell rings, since she teaches in the afternoon.

"Wednesday Wilson," she says, looking at my library card. "It's nice to meet you!"

"That's me," I say, passing her the book.
"Nice to meet you, too."

Ms. Eleanor turns the book over in her hand and reads the back cover. "You know, I have *never* seen this book before," she tells me. "Let me know how it goes," she calls to me as I take the book and run back to our table. Lunchtime is going by fast, and we have to get this sample done.

Charlie opens the book and flips to page ten. Then he carefully cuts a rectangle out of the middle of the page. When we're all satisfied with the result, he cuts the same-sized rectangle out of the next few pages, sometimes doubling up pages to work faster. When he has cut through about fifty pages, he hands the book to me.

I'm amazed at how perfect it looks!
From the outside, you would think it's just
a cringy book that no one wants to read,
but then when you open it, it's really a
Secret Keeper!

"Now all we need to do is glue the pages
together, and voilà! A working prototype!"
I say.

"What's a prototype?" asks Amina.

"A prototype is a model of the thing
you're creating," I tell everyone.

In the few minutes before the bell rings, I check out another book from our pile. Ms. Eleanor is so happy to see me again, she gives me a bookmark. She makes the library kind of fun, and I almost feel bad for using the books for something other than reading.

We decide to make two really good prototypes: one to give to the Emmas and one to show our classmates.

Once everyone sees our Secret Keepers, the orders will start pouring in, I'm sure of it. I'm excited but also nervous. We don't have a ton of time to save me from the wrath of the Emmas. And I don't want to imagine what will happen if I deliver their Secret Keeper a moment too late.

CHAPTER 8
Getting It Done

The rest of the day goes by so fast that
the next time I look up, it's to see
Ms. Gelson holding her hand in the air
to get everyone's attention. It's time to
clean up already!

Ms. Gelson reminds the class about our
museum trip on Friday. "Don't forget to
bring in your money and signed permission
forms!" she says.

I couldn't be happier until Emmet appears
out of nowhere and says, "Tomorrow
morning, *or else*," and points to the teacher.
Then he walks back to his desk, where
Emma M. is now holding a paper towel

against her cheek whenever Ms. Gelson isn't looking.

Charlie and Amina wait with me after school in my usual spot where I meet Mister.

Amina wishes us luck as she heads off to after-school care. "This will totally work!" she says.

On the way home, I ask Charlie to clear his schedule for the rest of the week. "We'll need all hands on deck once the orders start pouring in. You, too, Mister." As much as I find Mister annoying, I'm actually really grateful for his help right now.

"But how are you going to get the rest of the books?" asks Mister. "The library only lets you check out ten at a time."

"Let's just get out of trouble with the Emmas first," I tell him. "Then we can worry about the orders later."

As we walk through the door, my mom calls out from the kitchen, "Hello, my loves!" She's laid out a snack of apple slices and leftover pizza. Charlie is the only one excited about the pizza, because for me and Mister, it's basically another food group. As usual, Mom is covered in different paint colors, and today she has a face mask hanging around her neck from spray painting.

She looks like a character from a science-fiction movie, which I think is embarrassing but Charlie thinks is cool.

"What are you working on this time, Phoebe?" asks Charlie. Charlie always calls my mom and my mum by their first names, Phoebe and Teresa.

"A humongous painting with every color in my studio," she explains. Then she kisses us each on the forehead, even Charlie, and calls Charlie's mom to tell her that he's hanging out at our place. It seems like forever before my mom finally goes back to her studio.

As soon as she's gone, we scarf down the rest of the snacks and run upstairs. We put in front of us the book with the already hollowed-out pages that still needs to be glued together. Since there's a lot to do, we decide on a production line that looks like this:

Charlie cuts the hole in the second book.

I glue the pages together.

Mister sits on the books until the glue dries.

The first Secret Keeper looks pretty good, and in no time we have both prototypes done. But while we're waiting for the glue to dry, the What-Ifs start coming my way. The What-Ifs usually come from Mister, who is really good at thinking about the worst-case scenario. Today it's not just Mister, but Charlie, too.

"What if Ms. Eleanor notices the books you sign out are overdue and tells Ms. Gelson?" asks Charlie.

"We have two whole weeks before that matters," I reply.

"What if we're late for school because of traffic and you don't deliver the Secret Keeper on time?" says Mister nervously.

"Mister," I tell him, "we walk to school. There won't *be* traffic."

"What if Ms. Gelson sees your name on the overdue list and tells your moms?" Charlie adds.

"Charlie, no one even reads these books anymore. No one will notice they're gone." He's still not sure.

"What if —" Mister starts. But I've had enough.

"What if we get abducted by giant eagles on the way to school, and they drop us in the middle of the ocean, where a boat comes to rescue us, but then we end up in Australia?" I ask them angrily. Then I stare at the two of them out of frustration.

"You guys need to STOP!"

"Wednesday?" says Mister quietly a few seconds after my explosion.

"WHAT NOW?" I yell, hoping they get the point.

"Well, ummm … it's four-fifteen," he tells me.

"Shoot!" I say. I might already be in trouble with my friends for yelling at them, and I'll be in even more trouble if I'm late to Mr. Wright's.

CHAPTER 9

The Wrong Time for Wright

There are some things about Mr. Wright you need to know before you judge him for being a little strange. Because he's not. And maybe I shouldn't have said that, because I bet you're not the judgy type anyway.

Let me start over.

Remember how I told you I have to help Mr. Wright bring in his groceries so I can get my allowance? It's not as straightforward as I made it seem. Mr. Wright has agoraphobia. It sounds like this: *ah-go-ro-fo-bee-ah*, and it means he's afraid to leave his house. Well, he's afraid of things that happen in new places or something like that, so he always stays home. And it's not like with you and me, how going to summer camp without a friend can make us nervous. It's a lot more serious.

Mr. Wright does everything he can to stay inside. One of those things is ordering his groceries online to be delivered at exactly 4:15 p.m. on Mondays. The delivery driver won't go inside, and Mr. Wright won't go outside, so that's where I come in.

"Hello, Wednesday!" says Mr. Wright from his living room window as I run up his front steps.

The delivery driver has just plopped down four bags on his front porch. I quickly sign for them, which Mr. Wright always lets me do, since it's good practice for all the important papers I'll have to sign someday.

I hear the familiar click of the door unlocking, then grab all four bags at once and push the door handle open with my elbow. I need to get this done fast. "Hi, Mr. Wright. I'm in a bit of a hurry toda—"

"Great to see you!" he says, coming over to help me with the bags. "One of my clients sent me something I think you and your brother will like! Let me see where I put the box …"

"That's okay, Mr. Wright," I tell him, even though I know it's cookies. Mr. Wright's job is doing the voice-over for TV commercials, right from his computer in his living room. He even does commercials for a cookie company and gets sent free cookies! Fortunately, the boxes fit through the mail slot.

"Nonsense! I insist," he says, looking around his kitchen. "It's the least I can do for my entrepreneurial friend!"

As I watch him, I picture Charlie and

Mister sitting in my room talking about how awful I was to them. Perhaps they're even considering giving up right this second.

"Aha!" Mr. Wright exclaims as he finds the box.

Sure enough, it's triple-chocolate-chunk-marshmallow-hazelnut cookies — the kind my moms would never even *think* of buying.

"Thank you for the cookies," I say, edging closer to the door. Mr. Wright doesn't notice.

"Any new business ideas you're working on these days?" he asks, dipping his cookie into a glass of chocolate milk. "One day I'll be telling the world about how I lived next to the famous entrepreneur Wednesday Wilson."

At that moment, I feel like laughing and crying at the same time. Laughing because at this point the idea that I will ever have a successful business seems like a big fat joke. And crying because I think I just majorly messed up with Charlie and Mister, the two people I need now the most.

"I'm trying out a new idea," I explain, "but it's not going well. And it's my fault. I owe some people an apology."

Mr. Wright pops the rest of the cookie into his mouth and slurps down his chocolate milk. I just know he's scanning his brain for one of his Mr. Wright-isms, which always start the same way.

"If there's one thing I've learned …" he finally says, "it's to never ruin an apology with an excuse."

I think about what Mr. Wright said as I run home. When I reach my bedroom, I hand Charlie and Mister some cookies and clear my throat.

"I'm sorry for getting so mad. And for getting you into this mess in the first place. I'm also scared this won't work."

"It's okay, Wednesday," says Charlie. "There's no one else I'd rather get into trouble with."

"Wednesday," my mom calls out, "time for Charlie to leave for his swimming lesson!" We hear her walking up the stairs to my room. We're almost done, but I can't let her see all the cut-up pages from the library book on my bed, or she'll know something is up.

I throw myself over the mess just as she walks in.

"Aren't you going to walk your friend to the door?" she asks when I don't get up.

"Nope," I say.

"Pardon me, Wednesday?" she asks in her don't-even-think-about-repeating-what-you-just-said voice.

Charlie freezes and his face turns red. He blurts out, "Just like thumbprints, everyone's tongue prints are different!" Rushing past my mom, he calls out, "Thank you for having me, Phoebe!"

"Anytime, Charlie," she says, smiling after him. "You're always a pleasure."

I'm pretty sure Mom is about to tell me she's not amused when I'm saved by the Mum-joke we hear every day.

"Did somebody order a pizza?" Mum calls from her truck outside.

Mom laughs as usual and heads downstairs.

CHAPTER 10
The Ultimate Test

The next morning, I sneak downstairs and put the two completely finished Secret Keepers into a small metal box with a lid that locks shut. I may have had to empty out some of my mum's business-looking stuff, but I needed something that looks official.

Charlie is already waiting in the courtyard. I can tell he's nervous, because when Mister and I get to him, he starts to share a fact about volcanoes.

"Volcanoes can reach —"

"It's okay," I interrupt, opening the lid so he can see the Secret Keepers. "I have the Secret Keepers right here, just like we planned."

Charlie takes one out, and I can tell he's even more impressed than last time he saw them. "The Emmas aren't going to kill you!" he says.

"And we're gonna be rich!" I answer.

"Win-win!" says Mister, and we all run the rest of the way to school, getting there way before the bell. When we arrive at the front door, Principal Webb is holding it open for all the students.

"Good morning, friends," she says, even though I'm 100 percent sure we're not friends. "What do you have in the box, Wednesday?"

"Oh, it's just something for sharing with the class," I tell her, which is not completely a lie.

"Is it alive?" she asks nervously.

"Far from it!" I answer. I learned my lesson after the caterpillar incident last year.

"Is it … dead?" she asks quietly.

"Don't worry, Principal Webb," says Charlie. "There's nothing in that box that will cause any trouble."

"Thank you, Charlie," she says. "That's a relief." Then she greets some other students, and we walk away as fast as we can. We meet up with Amina and hurry off to class.

"Good luck!" Mister calls after us.

Things are already looking up today, because we have five minutes to spare before the first bell. Amina looks at both Secret Keepers for one suited for the Emmas and decides on the one called *Rumor Rescue*. She places it on Emma M.'s desk. Then we wait.

It's not long before Emma M. enters the

classroom, followed by Ruby and the other Emmas. She's wearing a heart-shaped bandage on her cheek. She means business. Charlie and I watch as Emma M. picks up the book and examines it. She holds it up to the light and looks at it, turns it over in her hand and taps on it with her fingernail.

Ruby looks from Emma M. to me to Charlie to Amina, and back to me. Even she looks nervous. I see a glimmer of the old Ruby, but then it fades away really fast.

"I don't get it," Emma M. says. "Why do you think I would read some weird old book? You are officially in so much troub—"

"Open it!" says Ruby.

Emma M. opens the book slowly, as if something inside is going to jump out at her. When she realizes it's hollow, a huge smile spreads across her face. Well, huge for an Emma, so basically one corner of her mouth turns up.

"But," says Emmet, "does it actually work?"

Work?! I can't believe I didn't test the Secret Keeper! What kind of an entrepreneur doesn't test her product?

Emma A. hands a note to the bandaged-faced Emma M. "I was thinking that exact same thing," says Emma M. as she reopens the cover.

Amina shuts her eyes, and Charlie shifts from foot to foot. I cross my fingers behind my back.

Emma M. places the note in the hollowed-out part of the book, directly in the center. Then she closes the book. I hold my breath. The cover stays shut, with the note safely inside.

I want to high-five Charlie and Amina in slow motion.

Emma M. strokes her bandage and passes the Secret Keeper to Ruby for inspection. The first bell is due any second, and so is Ms. Gelson. The classroom starts filling up with people, and they crowd around us, asking a million questions.

Everyone falls silent as Ruby turns the book over. She places it on a stack of other books, and you'd never know it's a Secret Keeper.

"It's pretty good," Ruby says. Then I swear she winks, but it's so fast that I can't tell.

"Let me try!" says Emmet, snatching the book away from her. "I *knew* I needed one of these."

"Is that the only Secret Keeper?" asks Emma N.

"We have a whole selection of Secret Keepers ready for manufacturing," I tell the crowd, passing around the other prototype. "They're two dollars each to preorder, *for a limited time only.*" I heard that last part on a TV commercial but had no idea how well it would work. Everyone is pushing their way to the front to get a look.

"I don't have any money, Wednesday!" says Adam.

"Didn't you bring your money for the field trip?" says Althea, rummaging through her bag. She hands me two dollars, and Charlie writes her name down on the preorder list.

Then everyone starts searching their bags for the field-trip money their parents gave them. People left, right and center are giving me their money. Just before Ms. Gelson walks in the door, we have an order for every kid in the class, even the other Emmas! Then the second bell rings.

"Take your seats, everyone," Ms. Gelson says, looking over at Charlie, who is standing there in shock. I'm telling you, this couldn't have gone any better. *I'm really cut out for this business stuff,* I think to myself as I look at our money pile in my desk. I count forty-two dollars. Once we have a bunch of satisfied customers stashing their secrets, more orders will pour in. We're officially in business, and nothing can stop us now!

CHAPTER 11
Nothing Except ...

"Earth to Wednesday," says Charlie, interrupting my thoughts. "The recess bell rang!"

Mister catches up with us shortly after we leave the class, and by the time we're on the playground, the Emmas are showing off their Secret Keeper to everyone. I feel like a successful entrepreneur as I pull out my clipboard to take orders from other students. I mean, customers. It's the first time I'm using my clipboard for a list since becoming a business owner. I divide the list into two columns: one for name and the other for classroom. I don't even have time to eat my snack because I'm too busy writing down orders. Maybe we should raise the price to four dollars tomorrow.

After recess, Ms. Gelson tells the class to hand in their permission forms and four dollars for the field trip. The whole class is suspiciously quiet. Emma M. hands Ms. Gelson her signed form and four dollars. Then Randall hands in his form and two dollars without making eye contact. Althea and Lamar do the same. I can tell that Ms. Gelson knows something is up when she stops the line and asks who

else in the class has the full four dollars. Amina, Charlie and I raise our hands, which looks pretty suspicious.

My stomach turns from not eating at recess and *maybe* a bit from worrying about how there is forty-two dollars in my desk, and Ms. Gelson is about to be exactly forty-two dollars short for our field trip. It's not a coincidence she's going to like.

"Wednesday, Charlie, Amina and Emma," says Ms. Gelson quietly, "do you have anything to share with me?"

I glance around the room with a confused look, like I don't know what she's talking about. The rest of the class is silent. Charlie looks like he's going to burst.

"Cherophobia is the fear of being happy," Charlie says at the top of his lungs. The class starts laughing, and I know I need to act fast before Charlie gets into trouble.

"They had nothing to do with it," I tell Ms. Gelson. "It was all my idea." Charlie tries to protest, but luckily he can't get words out right now, so he's told to go sit down.

I try my best to explain where the missing money went, but it's difficult because I don't want to drag anyone else into this. When I get to the part about cutting up library books, Ms. Gelson winces.

Ms. Gelson tells me she's sorry, but I have to go to the office because school property was damaged. I already know this is my third strike. I hand the forty-two dollars over to Ms. Gelson, then stop to say goodbye to Morten on my way out.

"I thought it was a really good idea, Morten," I tell him. But as I walk downstairs to the office, I know I'm about to find out I'm wrong, as usual.

CHAPTER 12
Busted

When I get to the office, the secretary, Mrs. Dawson, tells me to sit down and wait. I can hear through the door that Principal Webb is talking to my mum on the phone. I know it's my mum because it's just about the time when her customers would be shouting out lunch orders, and Principal Webb says, "Pepperoni? No! *Wednesday!*" Even Mrs. Dawson thinks it's funny.

I wait another thirty-five minutes until the lunch bell rings, and then Ms. Gelson arrives. A few minutes later, my moms come rushing into the office. I feel horrible that my mum is missing her lunchtime pizza sales to be here.

Principal Webb opens her office door, and we all cram around her desk.

"Thank you for coming in on such short notice," she says to my moms, who nod their heads. My mom puts her arm around me, and my mum chooses not to sit down. Instead she paces around the room. Ms. Gelson sits on the windowsill.

"It seems that Wednesday has ended up with half of the field-trip money from her class," says Principal Webb.

Of course, everyone looks at me, thinking I stole the money, so I have to tell them the whole story — even the part about the flying kale.

When I'm done telling the story, all of the adults look at each other, and no one says anything. Principal Webb doesn't seem to understand the purpose of a Secret Keeper, and when I try to explain, I'm shushed by my mum.

"Wednesday," says Principal Webb, "could you share with us where the books came from to make these Secret Keepers?" Clearly she knows, because she's asking in that voice that adults use when they already know the answer.

"The library," I tell them.

No one seems impressed. In fact, my mum buries her head in her hands.

Maybe if I explain the situation, they will be on my side. "The books we chose had stereotypes in them, which Ms. Gelson taught us are bad," I explain. I nod at Ms. Gelson like she's already on my side. She half smiles. So does my mom, but no one says anything.

I keep going. "Those books were so old-fashioned," I say, looking at my moms. "In one book, it was only the girl characters who needed to be rescued — never the boys. If you think about it, I did a pretty responsible thing."

Now my mum is smiling, too, and has her hand on my shoulder.

"I appreciate that Ms. Gelson has done an excellent job on her lesson on stereotypes," Principal Webb says. "However, you vandalized school property for the sake of your craft project."

"*Business*," I correct her. Probably not the best time.

"Wednesday," Principal Webb continues, "a lot of what happened here is against the rules." She explains that the library books were damaged beyond repair. And that selling things on school property is not allowed. (When I ask about the sixth-grade winter bake sale last year, she gives me an Emma-worthy death glare.)

"Wednesday will pay for the books the library has lost, obviously," says my mum. I imagine my piggy bank's butt getting lighter.

"Yes," says my mom, "and she'll think long and hard about the differences between good and not-so-good decisions."

"And perhaps," adds Ms. Gelson, "Wednesday will need to apologize to Ms. Eleanor, even if the books were not … the best suited to our collection."

Principal Webb says she will talk to the Emmas and Ruby about how they behaved, even though that makes me nervous.

I agree with the adults. Then I work up the courage to say something. "I'm sorry for any trouble I caused," I tell everyone, "and I will pay to replace the books I ruined. But I don't think we should replace them with the same books, because they were *problematic*." That's another fancy word my mom taught me, and I can tell she's trying not to smile.

"Secret Keepers are my first business idea, and maybe the way everything happened wasn't the greatest, but I did learn tons of things for next time I start a business. And there will be a next time, that's a promise."

Then I walk out of the office and straight out of school, never to be seen around these parts again.

THE END

EPILOGUE*

Okay, I made up that last part. There was no walking off into the sunset. I really had to go back to class after Principal Webb said more stuff about being a leader and making choices that have a positive impact. Ms. Gelson told me she was disappointed that I almost ruined the field trip, and I had to apologize to the class. It was embarrassing, but I got it over with quickly.

*A fancy word for the REAL end

And you know what? People still want Secret Keepers! Charlie did the math, and after I pay to replace the two library books, I'll have about $13.50 left in my piggy bank to buy books from the thrift shop so no one can get mad at me for repurposing. Then I will use the profit to buy more used books and then sell those, and, well, you get the picture.

And those books I signed out of the library? They were not replaced with the same books. Ms. Eleanor set up a committee to choose new books for the library, and I'm on it. We meet in the library twice a month during free time to vote on titles Ms. Eleanor finds for us. If it sounds worse than detention, then

THE NEW
LIBRARY BOOK
COMMITTEE

I'm not explaining it right, because it's actually really fun. Charlie, Amina and Mister are on the committee with me. Imagine our surprise when on the first day, Ruby showed up to volunteer, too. Maybe someday she'll tell me why she decided to be friends with the Emmas in the first place. Or maybe not. Either way, I have a lot to look forward to. Especially since I'm closer to my next big business idea than I've ever been.

I can just feel it.

Acknowledgments*

Wednesday and Mister could not have come to life without the voices of my own children, Dario and Oakland, who are of mixed race (Black, Cherokee and white) and opened my eyes to the lack of representation in books for children. They spent countless hours adding their own voices to my manuscript to provide authenticity to my characters where I, as a white woman, fell short. I hope this story resonates with other kids and shows that everyone deserves to have themselves reflected in a book, no matter what.

*A fancy word for saying thank you

A big thank-you needs to be extended to the *real* Ms. Carrie Gelson for accepting me into her classroom to observe her magical ways and for telling me to write for this age group in the first place. I may be a grown-up, but I will always listen to my teachers — especially Alison Acheson and Susin Nielsen from the University of British Columbia Creative Writing program.

Thank you to my agent, Claire Anderson-Wheeler, at Regal Hoffmann, for believing in Wednesday from the get-go; to Morgan Goble for her enormous talent; and to my editor, Katie Scott, and the whole Kids Can Press team for making this dream come true.

Bree Galbraith is a writer and graphic designer who lives with her family in Vancouver, British Columbia. Her critically acclaimed picture books include *Nye, Sand and Stones, Usha and the Stolen Sun* and *Milo and Georgie.* Bree holds a Masters in Creative Writing from the University of British Columbia. Visit breegalbraith.com to learn more.

Morgan Goble has been drawing since she could first hold a crayon. A graduate of the Bachelor of Illustration program at Sheridan College, Morgan lives with her husband and their cat, Noni, in Oakville, Ontario. *Wednesday Wilson Gets Down to Business* is her first children's book. To learn more about Morgan, visit morgangoble.ca.

WEDNESDAY WILSON

MORE ADVENTURES TO COME!